CHILLERS

Ghost from the Sea

ELEANOR ALLEN

Illustrated by
LEANNE FRANSON

PUFFIN BOOKS

CHILLERS

The Blob Tessa Potter and Peter Cottrill
Clive and the Missing Finger Sarah Garland
The Day Matt Sold Great-grandma Eleanor Allen and Jane Cope
The Dinner Lady Tessa Potter and Karen Donnelly
Fire Raiser! Philip Wooderson and Jane Cope
Freak Out! John Talbot
Ghost from the Sea Eleanor Allen and Leanne Franson
Ghost Riders Alex Gutteridge and Barry Wilkinson
The Haunting of Nadia Julia Jarman and Michael Charlton
Hide and Shriek! Paul Dowling
Jimmy Woods and the Big Bad Wolf Mick Gowar and Barry Wilkinson
Madam Sizzers Sarah Garland
The Mincing Machine Philip Wooderson and Dee Shulman
The Nearly Ghost Baby Delia Huddy and David William
The Real Porky Philips Mark Haddon
Sarah Scarer Sally Christie and Claudio Muñoz
Spooked Philip Wooderson and Jane Cope
Wilf and the Black Hole Hiawyn Oram and Dee Shulman

PUFFIN BOOKS

Published by the Penguin Group
Penguin Books Ltd, 27 Wrights Lane, London W8 5TZ, England
Penguin Books USA Inc., 375 Hudson Street, New York, New York 10014, USA
Penguin Books Australia Ltd, Ringwood, Victoria, Australia
Penguin Books Canada Ltd, 10 Alcorn Avenue, Toronto, Ontario, Canada M4V 3B2
Penguin Books (NZ) Ltd, Private Bag 102902, NSMC, Auckland, New Zealand

On the worldwide web at: www.penguin.com

Penguin Books Ltd, Registered Offices: Harmondsworth, Middlesex, England

First published by A&C Black (Publishers) Ltd 1995
Published in Puffin Books 1996
5 7 9 10 8 6 4

Set in Meridien

Made and printed in England by William Clowes Ltd, Beccles and London

British Library Cataloguing in Publication Data
A CIP catalogue record for this book is available from the British Library

ISBN 0-140-3741-2

Chapter One
Was She Pushed?

Clare wanted to SCREAM. Scream so loud, the walls would crack and the roof fall in. She threw back her head, opened her mouth and – couldn't! Nothing at all came out.

She struggled and pulled. There was a ripping sound. A button flew off her dungarees and she shot forward. Free. She skidded across the landing and hit the banister rail. She grabbed at it and half stumbled, half fell down the steep cottage stairs.

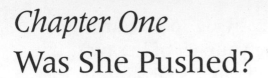

The door to the living room burst open and Simon, the younger of her two brothers, looked out. "'s'OK, Mum," he shouted. "'s'just Skirtie falling downstairs. Falling over her big, flat feet."

Then Dan appeared, grinning. He was her big brother.

Poor Skirtie hurtie? No. No damage done. Luckily she landed on her HEAD!
OK love? What happened?
I fell down the stairs.
They are steep. You need to be more careful.
I'm OK. I've taken the skin off my elbow, that's all.

“And you’ve popped the button off your dungarees.” Mum said as she flipped the strap which was now hanging loose. “Come and sit down.”

Clare didn’t tell them what had happened upstairs. She just went and sat in a chair by the fire. Mum made her a mug of sweet tea.

Clare was glad she hadn’t screamed. They’d have wanted to know why, and she would have had to invent a lie. She couldn’t have told the truth. Not in front of Dan and Simon. No way.

Dan would have laughed himself silly. As for Simon, he'd have been up those stairs with his zapper gun faster than you could mutter "Ghostbusters". Clare winced at the thought.

Her hands shook as she glanced up at the dark rafters of the long, low room. She pricked up her ears for sounds from above. Her back prickled and she could feel the hair on her head rising as she listened. But she knew she would have to keep this to herself.

Chapter Two
What a Stink!

It was because of Clare they were staying at Beachcomber Cottage. She'd had a bad bout of flu and Mum had decided a breath of sea air would do her good. They'd booked the cottage for the weekend of February half-term. Dad had stayed at home because he was working.

Mum! Simon hit me!
Are we there sooon?
Mum! I'm hungry!
MUM! Dan took my Ghostbuster!
Did not!
Mum!

The journey had been really long and tedious. Clare and her brothers had squabbled constantly and made their mother angry.

They all arrived tired and irritable – and in a mist. They couldn't see the sea, or much of anything else. The cottage in the cove didn't look a bit like the sun-baked one in the brochure.

It smells in here.
It's all damp and musty! Gross!
What a place! We should've stayed at home!
Well, we could've done B&B if you lot weren't so noisy!

"I'll put the kettle on," Mum said, trying to sound cheerful and organised. "You lot get the cases in."

Clare grabbed her stuff from the boot. While the boys were still messing about, she hauled it up the steep cottage stairs. There was a narrow landing at the top, with just two doors leading off it. The bathroom was downstairs, added on at the back. The brochure had said there was a double bed in the front bedroom and she and Mum had agreed to share it.

They'd all thought the cottage smelled musty downstairs. That was April fresh compared to this!

It wasn't just a smell, it was more of a stench! Clare was reminded of Dan's football socks, when he'd left them festering in a plastic bag over the Christmas holiday. The stench was nearly the same – only there was more of it. Much more of it.

She heard bangs and shouts and pushings and shovings as the boys stumbled their way up the stairs.

"In here. And the name's Clare," she added, automatically.

She turned to them, her face screwed up in revulsion, waiting for their gasps to start. The "Phaugh!" and the "Cor, what a pong!" and the "What a whiff!"

WOW! Look at the view!
ACE! The mist's gone. You can see out to sea for MILES!

View? Clare spun round as they barged past her towards the window. It was true about the view. There was a sweep of dark, grey-green sea that might have taken her breath away, if she hadn't been gasping already.

What about the SMELL? They didn't seem to have noticed it. Incredible!

This room's great. Let's bag it!
Mum and I are in here.
You didn't want to share a double bed...

Clare muttered, suddenly less keen to stake a claim. Whoever slept in here would be in danger of asphyxiation.

We don't have to. What do you call that, Cross-eyes?
You have that folding bed, Simon. I'll have THIS!

The bed Dan had thrown himself on to had a big brass bedstead. It looked as if it had stood in the room for a hundred years or more. Clare didn't like it. She certainly didn't fancy sleeping in it. And could that be where the foul smell was coming from?

Eugh! It wasn't fading. Clare put a hand across her mouth. If she stayed in that room another minute, she'd be sick.

"Can't you–?"

Dan cut her off.

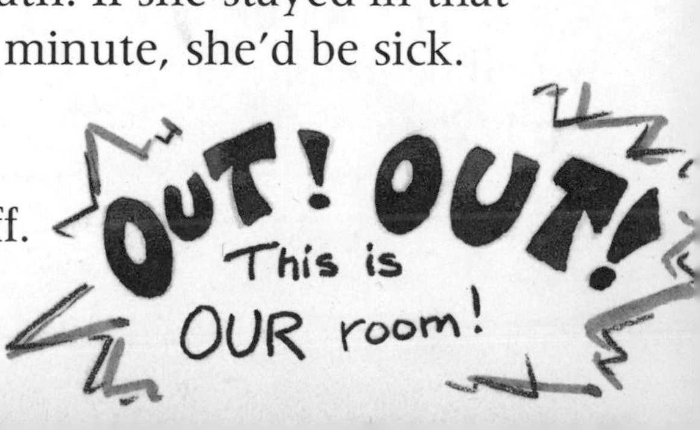

OUT! OUT!
This is OUR room!

He pushed her to the
door and shoved
her through.

Clare wasn't a wimp.
But this time she didn't struggle. She was glad to gasp the fresh air on the landing.

Slowly, she walked to the back bedroom. Cautiously, she looked in. No spectacular view, just the cliff-face with coarse tufts of grass growing out of it. No brass bedstead – only a couple of modern wooden bunk beds. No nasty smell.

She listened to her brothers crashing around in the front room, bouncing on the bed. They obviously still hadn't noticed any awful smell.

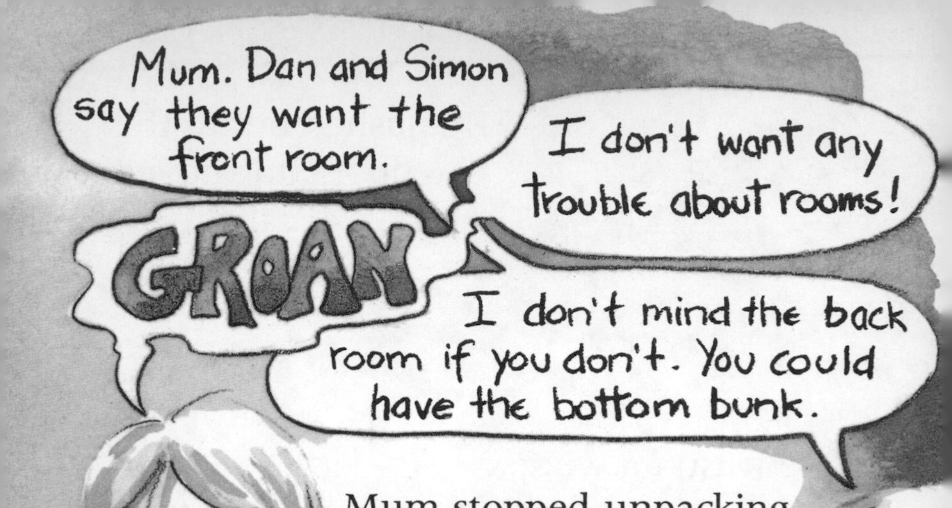

Mum. Dan and Simon say they want the front room.
I don't want any trouble about rooms!
GROAN
I don't mind the back room if you don't. You could have the bottom bunk.

Mum stopped unpacking the food and pondered. "The front room has a double bed. No way are those two sharing a bed. They'd be fighting and kicking each other out of it all night."

"There's a folding bed for Simon to sleep on. Dan says he wants the double bed to himself. I'd rather sleep on the top bunk."

Mum raised her eyebrows. "Are you telling me everybody's in agreement?"

"Yes, if it's all right by you."

She shrugged. "It's all right by me I guess. I'll be so tired, I won't care where I sleep."

Clare put her mother's suitcase in the back room with hers. Then she stuck a chair against the door. If Dan and Simon suddenly nosed in to the stench, there was no way they were going to oust her. She needn't have worried. A minute or two later, Mum shouted and she heard the pair of them clattering back down the stairs.

Drinks are ready!
OK, Mum! Coming!
Why can't those two SMELL anything? It's really starting to bug me!

She decided to go up after tea and check the front room again, but she forgot. There were so many interesting things to look at in the living room. There were maps on the walls showing shipwrecks; old jigsaw puzzles in the cupboard; lots of books about smugglers, legends and natural history; and piles of old surfing magazines.

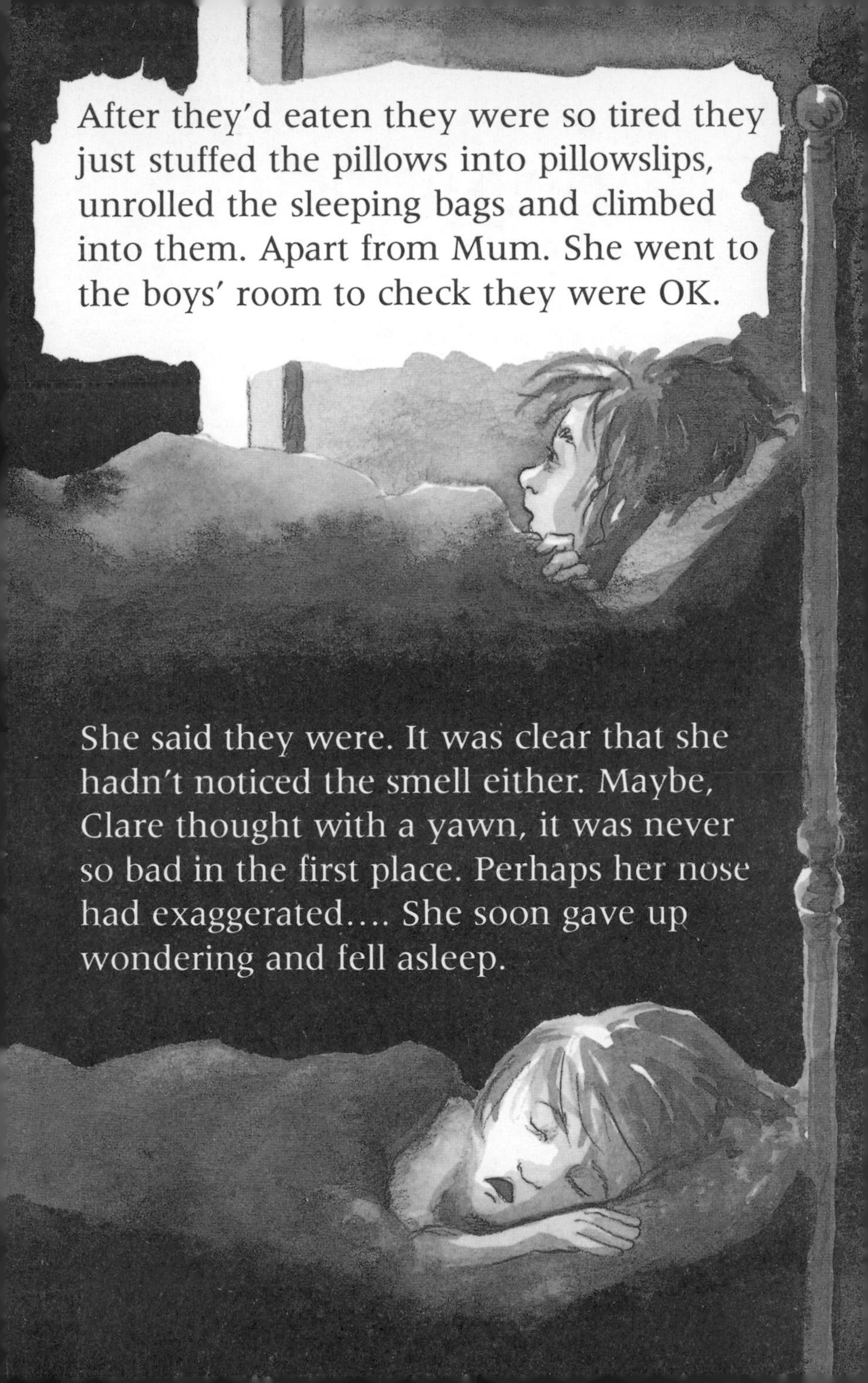

After they'd eaten they were so tired they just stuffed the pillows into pillowslips, unrolled the sleeping bags and climbed into them. Apart from Mum. She went to the boys' room to check they were OK.

She said they were. It was clear that she hadn't noticed the smell either. Maybe, Clare thought with a yawn, it was never so bad in the first place. Perhaps her nose had exaggerated.... She soon gave up wondering and fell asleep.

Chapter Three
Ghost From the Sea

Next day, it was bright and sunny. They stayed out all day, visiting sandy beaches, picnicking on the clifftop, and getting plenty of the fresh sea air that they had driven all that way for.

It was late afternoon when they arrived back at the cottage. As dusk was falling, the boys went to explore along the lane.

Mum opened the door and as Clare smelt the musty interior, she remembered the mysterious smell in the front bedroom. She decided to check it out again, whilst the boys' backs were turned.

As soon as she'd taken off her anorak and boots, she dashed upstairs.

Her memory hadn't exaggerated – it had UNDERrated! The smell was enough to knock you off your feet. And it WAS coming from the big brass bed!

Clare froze – shocked rigid. Somebody was lying on the bed!

The big, dark, shadowy mound of a man was there.

She saw a beard, a wild, grey beard, and a big knitted jersey, coarse trousers and thick, rough socks. Beside the bed stood a great, damp-looking pair of boots.

He was breathing heavily and grunting as he did so. Fast asleep. The smell was rising from *him* and drifting in sickening waves across the room.

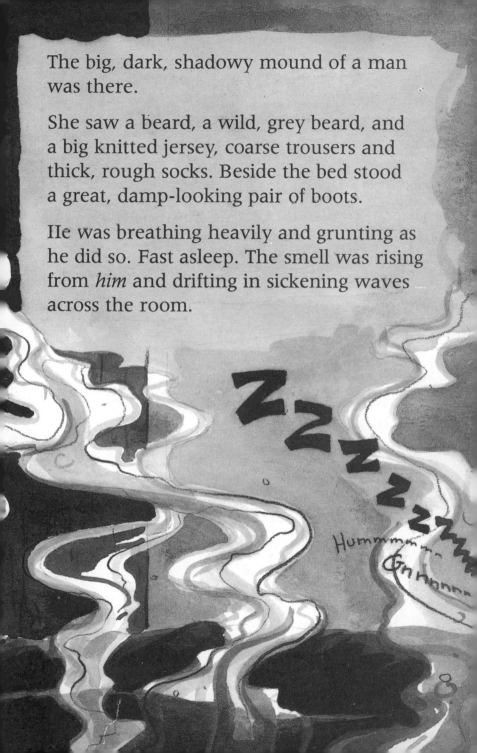

Where had he come from? What was he doing in *their* cottage? Had he broken in? Clare's heart seemed to stop beating, then start up again with a great thump, as if it were trying to burst out of her chest.

He didn't look like a robber. He looked more like a seaman. An old-fashioned seafarer, like those she'd seen in the books downstairs. A seafarer, she noticed now, with a strange peculiarity – one eyebrow glowing pure white against his weather-beaten skin.

She felt the bitter taste of vomit in her mouth. Her brain had suddenly added a frightening thought.

Maybe it isn't just the smell of sweat from years at sea. Maybe it's the smell of DEATH!

Cor-Skirtie! You scared the living daylights out of me! I thought you were a GHOST standing there!
What do you think you're doing in OUR room? Skulking around in the dark in OUR room!

The light shot on, dazzling Clare's eyes and shocking her out of her trance.

It was an exaggeration to say it was dark, but it had been dim and shadowy.

LOOK!
No! YOU look.
Keep out of our room
Or we'll come
and raid yours.
YES! Or
we'll raid yours.
So THERE!

Simon shouted as he crossed the room to fling himself on his folding bed. Dan went to stand by the window. Neither of them had noticed – HIM.

Clare's eyes flew back to the bed.

He wasn't there anymore.

"I feel sick!" she groaned and flew downstairs to the loo.

After being so ill, perhaps you've overdone things a bit today.

Clare didn't contradict her. Maybe she should have tried to explain, to Mum at least. But downstairs, in the warmth of the living room, she wanted to believe that perhaps she HAD been overtired, and in the dusk had seen a shadow and let her imagination run riot.

In the middle of the night Clare woke up in a panic. What if she had really seen him? At that moment Dan was sleeping in the big brass bed. The seadog's bed! What if... It didn't bear thinking about!

Clare seemed to be awake for hours, her ears pricked for any ominous noises coming through the wall. But she didn't hear a thing. Eventually she fell asleep.

When she woke up again, the only smell was a reassuring one – toast.

She pulled on her dungarees and hurried downstairs.

Dan and Simon were already sitting at the table, stuffing themselves and talking to each other in stupid voices. Their normal, abnormal selves.

Did you sleep all right?
What?!
Doesn't matter.

HEY! Dan shouted as Clare reached for the last piece of toast.

That's mine. Hands OFF!
I made that!
You didn't.
The Toaster did!
Make YOUR OWN!
MEAN PIG.

Why had she worried about him? She poked out her tongue. Serve Dan right if a great, ghostly seaman had lowered his smelly carcass on the bed and sprawled out all over him… No, she thought, not even Dan deserved that.

Chapter Four
The *Matilda-Jane*

After breakfast, whilst the boys were doing a jigsaw puzzle and their mother was making sandwiches, Clare slipped up to the front bedroom.

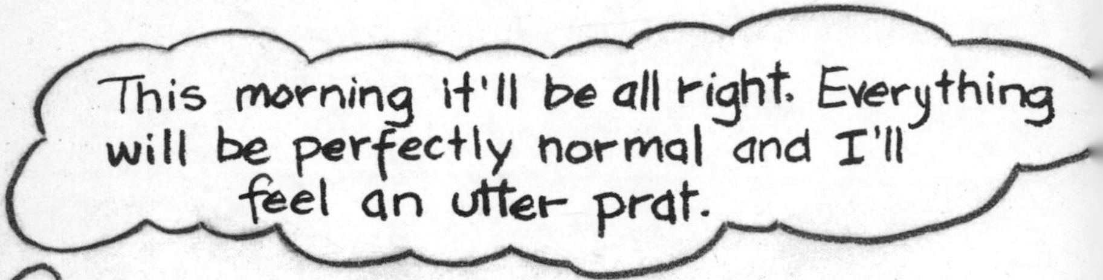

This morning it'll be all right. Everything will be perfectly normal and I'll feel an utter prat.

She had convinced herself it *was* a shadow she'd seen – that he wouldn't be there. Confidently, she pushed open the door…

Lying on the bed in the full glare of morning light, just like before, was the seaman!

No – not quite like before!

Fear tore through Clare, sharp and spiralling like a corkscrew, as she realised there was one big difference.

His eyes flickered open and he was staring straight at her from beneath that strange white brow. Then, slowly, he started to raise himself off the bed and swing his big, stockinged feet to the floor...

Clare panicked.

She flung herself at the door, a fearful scream sticking in her throat. As she tried to stumble through, something happened that reduced her to a frenzy.
She couldn't move!

She could feel herself being pulled backwards by the strap of her dungarees. He'd caught her!

She tried again to scream – for help this time. But the scream shrivelled and died. She struggled and pulled. Suddenly, there was a snapping sound. She shot forward on to the landing and down the stairs.

It was then she was given sweet tea and sympathy by her mother, who thought she'd slipped and fallen…

Get a move on if you've finished your tea, Clare. We don't want to waste our last day hanging around the cottage. Go up and change into your jeans. You can't walk around with the strap of your dungarees dangling loose.

How could she go back up there? But the moment for blurting out the truth to her mother had now passed.

As she stared up at the rafters, Clare wondered if he was still up there, waiting to grab her... Why would he have done that? Ghosts don't usually attack people. Usually, they just scare the living daylights out of you so your hair turns white and you turn into a quivering, jibbering mass.

"And you two," Mum added. "Go up and get your sweaters."

Dan and Simon too. What a relief!

She tagged along, close behind. They were arguing as they entered the front bedroom. But for once she was glad to hear their noisy, boisterous voices. No chance of any ghostly happenings with those two around!

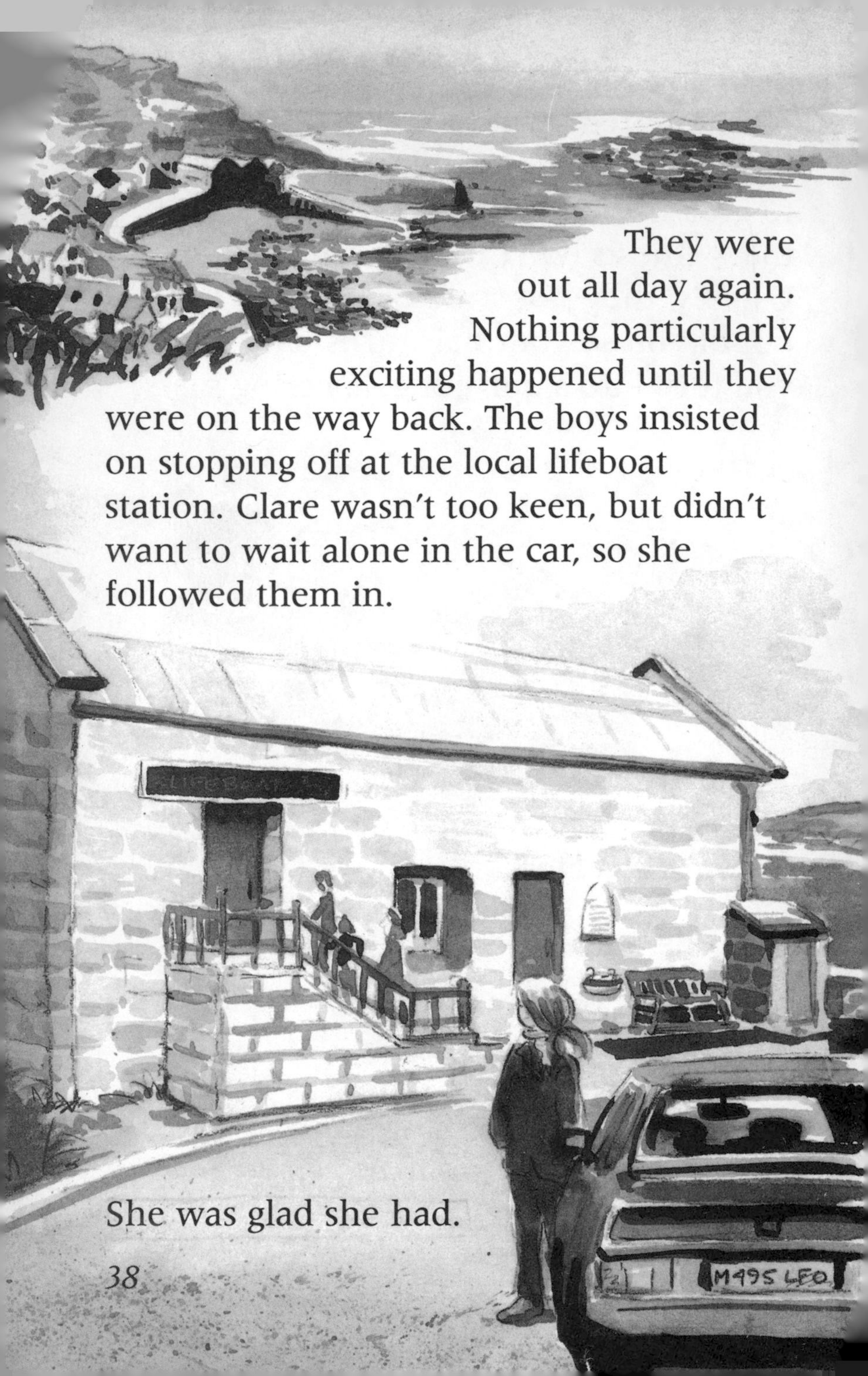

They were out all day again. Nothing particularly exciting happened until they were on the way back. The boys insisted on stopping off at the local lifeboat station. Clare wasn't too keen, but didn't want to wait alone in the car, so she followed them in.

She was glad she had.

In the centre of the shed was the lifeboat, the new *Matilda-Jane*, painted dark blue, gleaming and very ship-shape. Around the walls were lots of charts and photographs. There were photos of wrecked, tall-masted ships with names like *Black-Eyed Susan*, *Bosphorus* and *Normandy*; photos of former lifeboats being launched, lifeboats that were rowed by oars and hauled down to the water on long,

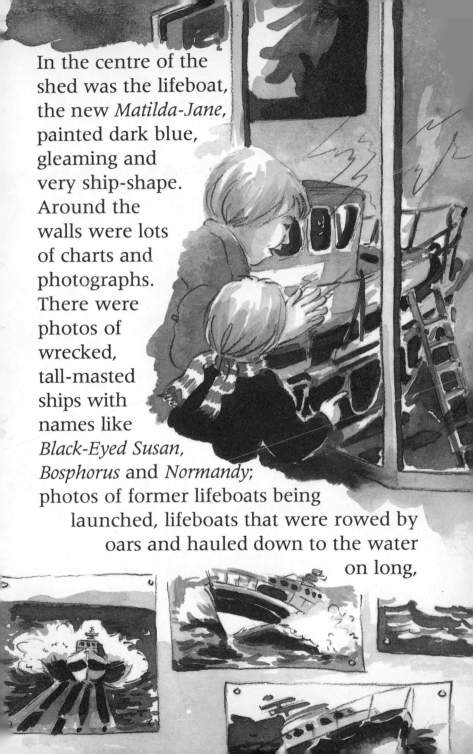

low carriages with wheels; photos of the crews wearing sou'wester hats and big, cumbersome life-jackets made of cork...

A sudden chill shot through Clare. Was it excitement? Amazement? Fear? A mixture of all, she decided.

read the caption.

Big men in fishermen's jumpers, coarse trousers and heavy boots posed proudly beside the boat. Clare searched eagerly:

Walter Killigrew, Coxswain.
No doubt about it. The beard was neater, the face was glowing with health, but the one eyebrow was white – pure white!

Clare's ghostly seafarer was a real person. A man with a name.

Walter Killigrew, Coxswain of the *Matilda-Jane* in 1882. That was who he was.

Clare moved shakily on to the next photo. It showed a wreck, the *Rutland* that had been lost in a hurricane. Sixteen of the crew had perished, despite the gallant attempt of the *Matilda-Jane* to save them.

Clare pictured the lifeboatmen on the little *Matilda-Jane*, struggling with oars through the terrific seas. Was that when Walter Killigrew had met his end? Clare read the caption again. No mention of any lifeboatman lost.

The next photo showed the crew of the *Matilda-Jane* in 1884, at the time the *Rutland* went down.

Coxswain: Samuel Bottrell. Where is Walter Killigrew? What happened to him?
's boring in here. And I'm STARVING! Let's go home.

Clare opened her mouth to protest. But she changed her mind and followed the rest of the family back to the car. No point in begging for more time. The next photo had jumped to 1891. So she wouldn't find out what had happened to Coxswain Killigrew from that.

Back at the cottage, Clare looked through all the books on local history, but there wasn't a single clue.

That night, lying in her bunk, she couldn't stop picturing the little lifeboat with its gallant crew rowing through the towering seas to save the crew of the *Rutland*. It had been a sad mission. Sixteen men had perished...

But what had happened to Walter Killigrew? Why wasn't he the coxswain in 1884? What had happened to him?

Again, Clare relived the dreadful moment when his ghost had risen from the bed and grabbed her by the strap of her dungarees....
Why? she asked herself. Why?

Then she began to feel very guilty again about not warning Dan and Simon. If Walter Killigrew had tried to get her in broad daylight, what might he do to them, in the dark. Especially to Dan, sleeping innocently in the brass bed.

It's a good thing we're going home tomorrow. I don't think I could bear another night here.

Clare felt worn out when she woke next morning.

Outside, it was blowing a gale. Rain lashed against the windows and wind rattled the panes.

But it didn't matter. Nothing about this place matters any more, she told herself. In another hour or so, they'd be safely away from the cove, Beachcomber Cottage, and the mystery of Walter Killigrew.

She packed her things to take downstairs with her, so she would not have to come back up for them.

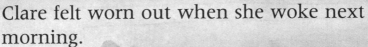

As she was putting her luggage on to the landing, she noticed the button off her dungarees glinting in the corner. She bent to pick it up, and glanced nervously towards the front bedroom. There was no sound, no movement. Still she felt her skin prickle.

She looked at the old-fashioned door handle. Suddenly, something jarred in her mind – something she had only half-registered in the frenzy of that moment yesterday. In her mad panic to get out of the room, could she have caught her strap on that handle? Was it the door handle that had held her back?

A guilty flush spread over Clare's cheeks as she went over those ghastly seconds and realised what could have happened.

Maybe the ghost of Walter Killigrew had never left the bed at all? Maybe, he had never meant her any harm? Maybe, apart from petrifying anybody who could see him, and rotting their nasal passages, he was incapable of doing harm? Maybe, he was just THERE, locked into another dimension, like a sort of time-traveller?

Her mother had said that when you've been ill and you're still run-down, your resistance is low. Maybe, thought Clare, all your senses are heightened in some way, and you can see and feel and smell things that otherwise you wouldn't. Maybe that was why *she* could see and smell the ghost and nobody else could?

Chapter Five
Seafarer's Boots

The rain stopped after breakfast, but the wind was still blowing hard. Great breakers crashed against the sea wall, and they were almost lifted off their feet as they packed the car. A maroon alarm had gone off earlier, startling them with its bang. Their mother had said it meant there must be a ship in distress. Clare could see she was worried about setting off in such a strong wind, but it might keep up all day and she wanted to be home before dark.

At last, Mum locked the cottage door behind them and they piled into the car.

Looks like they're launching the lifeboat.
Cor! Can we get out and watch?
No time. Sorry. ... OK everybody? Ready for off?
No! Hang on a minute!

There were groans all round as Clare started to climb out of the car. Mum said, "Where are you going?"

"Er – I forgot my diary," Clare lied.

More groans. She'd recently started keeping a diary and was sure Dan and Simon had plans to steal and read it. "I hid it under the carpet in our room," she added. "Where THEY couldn't find it."

Mum sighed and dangled the keys. "OK – be quick about it!"

Clare ran back into the cottage, dashed up the stairs, and headed straight towards the front bedroom.

From the minute the maroon had gone off after breakfast, she'd had a peculiar feeling – a sort of uneasy excitement churning at her insides. When she was in the car, looking at the cottage for the last time, the feeling had grown stronger. Then, as soon as her mother mentioned the lifeboat, Clare was half out of the car before she knew what she was doing.

Whatever was drawing Clare back into Beachcomber Cottage, it was far, far more powerful than her fear. She took a deep breath, then peered round the door.

The ghost of Walter Killigrew was there, lying on the bed.

This time Clare didn't feel scared. Perhaps it was because she knew now he would do her no harm.

His eyes flickered open. He started to raise himself off the bed. But she didn't run. She had to know what he wanted.

It was as if she were seeing a play on stage. Like watching a scene that the old seaman had been acting out, time after time, for more than a hundred years.

He swung his stockinged feet to the floor, then leant forward, reaching towards his boots. Those big, damp-looking seafarer's boots that stood on the mat beside the bed. He faltered and seemed to turn faint. Again, he tried to reach out for the boots, but they were beyond his reach.

He collapsed back on to the bed with a great, shuddering sigh.

Clare felt his need, his overpowering need, to get those boots. She'd no idea why he needed them. She just knew that, through all the years, he had been trying to reach them but never had the strength. She also knew he would never give up. Until he did reach them, his spirit could never rest.

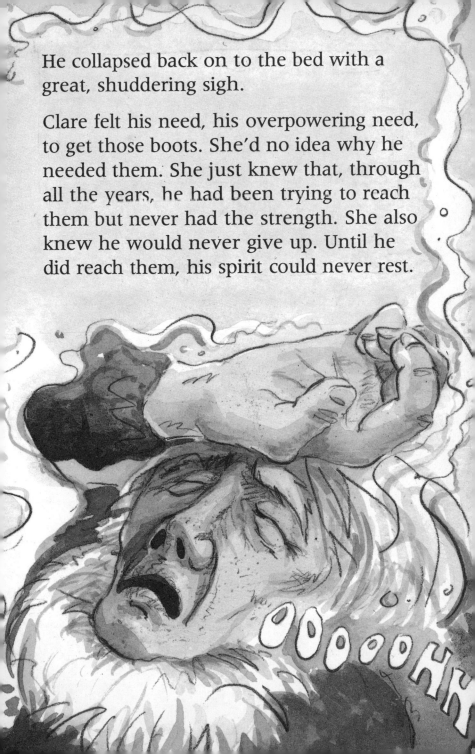

What could she do?

Clare moved forward, stealthily. Afraid that if she reached out to pick them up, the boots would disappear.

She hardly dared to breathe as she felt the cold, damp leather beneath her fingers. She lifted, expecting them to be heavy, and was surprised to feel no weight. She placed the boots carefully on the bed beside the seaman, just within his reach. Then she backed towards the door.

He rose up again. He reached out for the boots and his fingers fastened round them. For a second or two he hugged them to his chest.

Then slowly, he struggled them on to his feet.

An enormous feeling of relief flooded through Clare.

She heard the old seafarer give a sigh. It wasn't a sad sigh. It was the sigh of a soul that has just been put out of its torment.

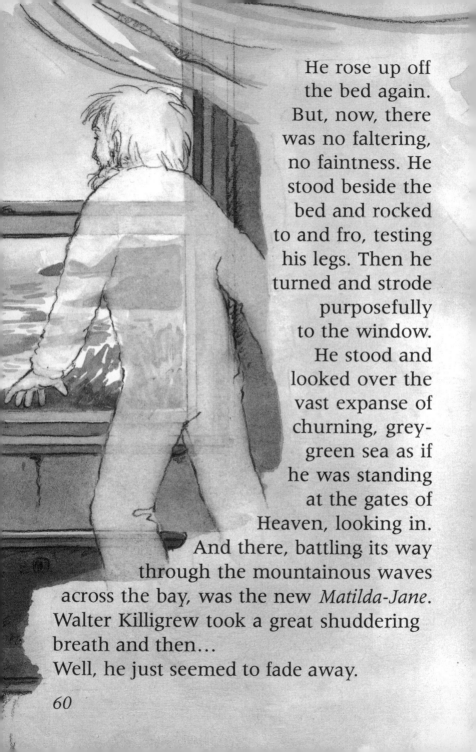

He rose up off the bed again. But, now, there was no faltering, no faintness. He stood beside the bed and rocked to and fro, testing his legs. Then he turned and strode purposefully to the window. He stood and looked over the vast expanse of churning, grey-green sea as if he was standing at the gates of Heaven, looking in. And there, battling its way through the mountainous waves across the bay, was the new *Matilda-Jane*. Walter Killigrew took a great shuddering breath and then...

Well, he just seemed to fade away.

He disappeared! This time Clare knew it was for good. A sudden shaft of sunlight flickered across the bed where he had been lying and the room smelt fresh and clean.

And now, at last, Clare understood.

Walter must have been ill, dying maybe, on that memorable day in 1884 when the first *Matilda-Jane* had been called to the rescue of the *Rutland*. He'd heard the call and tried to obey it. He had tried to summon up enough strength to lead his crew, but had failed.

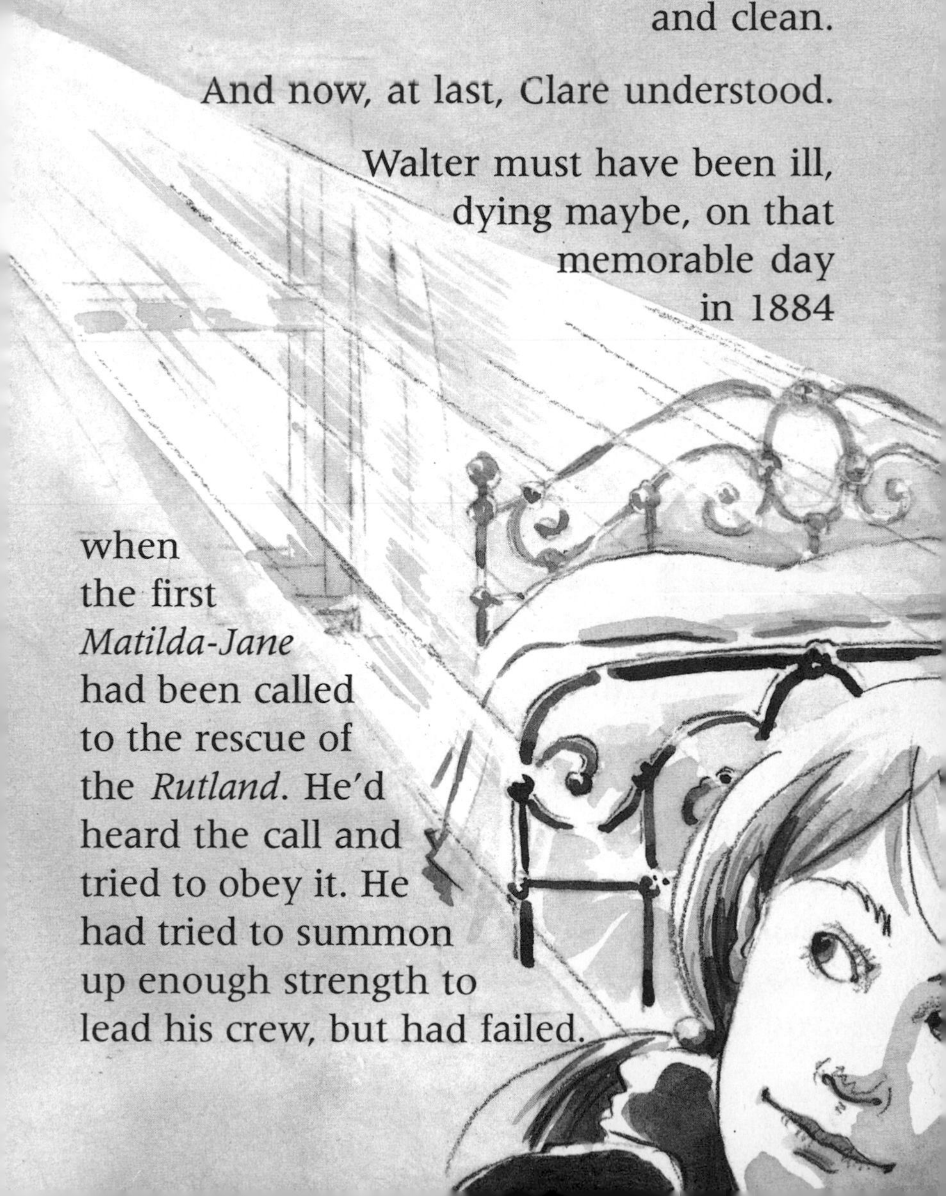

Through the window he had watched the lifeboat fighting across the bay with a reserve, Samuel Bottrell, in his place. But, despite the "gallant attempt" of the *Matilda-Jane,* sixteen seamen had died. If Walter had been able to get off that bed, pull his boots on and lead his crew, might the outcome have been different?

Clare went to the window and watched the little lifeboat as it fought its way slowly round the headland. She waved it goodbye and wished it luck. She knew its good luck was certain because, after more than a hundred years of trying in vain, the spirit of Coxswain Killigrew was free and on board the new *Matilda-Jane.*

Then, to sound authentic, she added, "Unless you've stolen it!"

"Cor – you're so STUPID, Skirtie!"

"What a laugh!" jeered Dan. "Why would WE want to read YOUR diary? Bet it says things like, 'Today, I played with my Sindy dolls.' Bet it's a load of ”

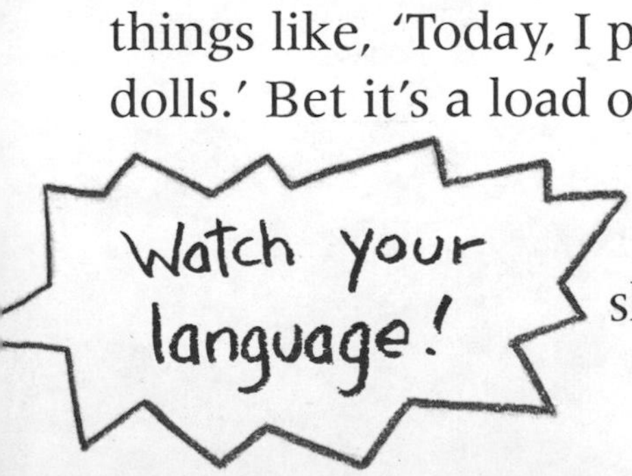

shouted their mother.

And so, squabbling noisily, they drove away, leaving Beachcomber Cottage and its memories, silently waiting until another family arrived to shatter the peace.

Clare settled down thoughtfully for the long journey home, whilst on the back seat, Simon whooshed and zapped with his Ghostbusters. Dan said he ought to grow up, because, "There's no such things as ghosts."